George and the New Craze

by Alice Hemming

illustrated by Kimberley Scott

There was a new craze at the Wildlife Park. Everyone had cards with pictures of people on them!

The penguins had a full set
of People Cards.

George had three People Cards.

He was very happy with them – even though two of the cards were the same.

Gilbert

Gilbert is a lorry driver. He also plays the drums in a band.

Gilbert

Gilbert is a lorry driver. He also plays the drums in a band.

Sonia

Sonia is a hairdresser, and she loves to sing karaoke.

Sid had one card.

It was a rare card.

"What are People Cards for?" Sid asked.

"I don't know," said George.

George and Sid tried to make
a tower. That didn't work.

They tried to play Snap.
That didn't work.

They put the cards in a big book.

There were lots of gaps.

They needed more cards.

"Shall we look for more People Cards?"
said George.
"No," said Sid. He liked his one rare
card.

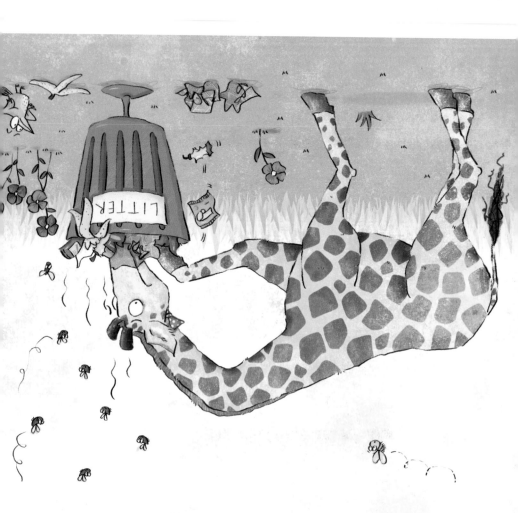

George found a card.

It was a bit mucky, so he cleaned it up.

George bumped into Toni.

Toni was also looking for cards.

"Shall we share our cards?"
said George.

So they did.

So did Gus.

And Mo and Max.

And Minnie.

All together, they had lots of cards.

They made a big tower.

They played lots of games of Snap.

But they needed one more card to
fill up the book.

"I will share my rare card," said Sid.

Gilbert

Gilbert is a lorry driver. He also plays the drums in a band.

Alice

Alice is an author. She likes rainy days.

Filippo

Filippo is a librarian. He has travelled to hundreds of different countries.

Clara

Clara is a schoolgirl. Her favourite animal is a platypus.

Mara

Mara is a horse rider. She loves to ride and care for her horses.

The Queen

The Queen wears a shiny crown. She enjoys summer garden parties.

Sonia

Sonia is a hairdresser, and she loves to sing karaoke.

Rajit

Rajit is a veterinary surgeon. He bakes a lovely raspberry cheesecake.

Tommy

Tommy is a little boy. He rides his bike super-fast.

Babette

Babette is a security guard. Her favourite colour is green.

Steve

Steve is a publisher. He wears extremely colourful shirts.

Kimberley

Kimberley is an illustrator. She likes to do Yoga and stand on her head.

Everyone was happy. Sid was glad
he had shared his card.

"Come and show the penguins!"
said George.

But the penguins had finished
with People Cards.

They had started a new craze.

Marbles!

Quiz

1. What is the first new craze at Heavenly Hippos Wildlife Park?
a) Hats
b) People Cards
c) Marbles

2. Who has the rare card?
a) George
b) Sid
c) Toni

3. What colour is the rare card?
a) Gold
b) Blue
c) Pink

4. How many cards are there altogether?

a) One

b) Three

c) One hundred

5. What game do they play with the cards?

a) Snap

b) Happy families

c) Guess the card

Turn over for answers

Pink

Red (End of Yr R)

Yellow

Blue

Green

Orange

Turquoise (End of Yr 1)

Purple

Gold

White (End of Yr 2)

Lime

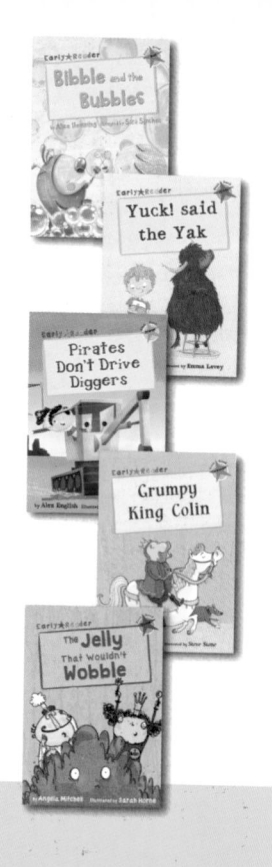

Book Bands for Guided Reading

The Institute of Education book banding system is made up of twelve colours, which reflect the level of reading difficulty. The bands are assigned by taking into account the content, the language style, the layout and phonics.

Children learn at different speeds but the colour chart shows the levels of progression with the national expectation shown in brackets. To learn more visit the IoE website: www.ioe.ac.uk.

Maverick early readers have been adapted from the original picture books so that children can make the essential transition from listener to reader. All of these books have been book banded for guided reading to the industry standard and edited by a leading educational consultant.

Quiz Answers: 1b, 2b, 3a, 4c, 5a